Thanks to Mom,
Dad, and Kirsten

ABOUT THIS BOOK • The illustrations for this book were rendered digitally. This book was edited by Andrea Spooner and designed by Véronique Lefèvre Sweet. The production was supervised by Erika Schwartz, and the production editor was Marisa Finkelstein. The text was set in Avenir LT Pro and Invention Hunters, and the display type is LunchBox and Rockwell. • Copyright © 2020 by Korwin Briggs • Cover illustration copyright © 2020 by Korwin Briggs. Cover design by Karina Granda and Véronique Lefèvre Sweet. Cover copyright © 2020 by Hachette Book Group, Inc. • Hachette Book Group supports the right to free expression and the value of copyright. The purpose of copyright is to encourage writers and artists to produce the creative works that enrich our culture. • The scanning, uploading, and distribution of this book without permission is a theft of the author's intellectual property. If you would like permission to use material from the book (other than for review purposes), please contact permissions@hbgusa.com. Thank you for your support of the author's rights.• Little, Brown and Company • Hachette Book Group• 1290 Avenue of the Americas, New York, NY 10104 • Visit us at LBYR.com • First Edition: July 2020 • Little, Brown and Company is a division of Hachette Book Group, Inc. • The Little, Brown name and logo are trademarks of Hachette Book Group, Inc. • The publisher is not responsible for websites (or their content) that are not owned by the publisher. • Library of Congress Cataloging-in-Publication Data • Names: Briggs, Korwin, author, illustrator. • Title: The Invention Hunters discover how light works / written and illustrated by Korwin Briggs. • Description: First edition. | New York ; Boston : Little, Brown and Company, 2020. | Series: The Invention Hunters ; [3] | • Summary: "When the Invention Hunters, a group of globe-trotting invention collectors, visit a school in their flying museum, a student helps them by explaining how common concepts related to light, like refraction, magnification, and reflection, and objects, like cameras and televisions, work"— Provided by publisher. • Identifiers: LCCN 2019001738| ISBN 9780316467964 (hardcover) | ISBN 9780316467988 (ebook) | ISBN 9780316467940 (library edition ebook) • Subjects: | CYAC: Light—Fiction. | Inventions—Fiction. • Classification: LCC PZ7.1.B7546 Im 2020 | DDC [E]—23 • LC record available at https://lccn.loc.gov/2019001738 • ISBNs: 978-0-316-46796-4 (hardcover), 978-0-316-46795-7 (ebook), 978-0-316-46798-8 (ebook), 978-0-316-46800-8 (ebook) • PRINTED IN CHINA • 1010 •
10·9 8 7 6 5 4 3 2 1

THE INVENTION HUNTERS

DISCOVER HOW LIGHT WORKS

Written and illustrated by

KORWIN BRIGGS

LITTLE, BROWN AND COMPANY

NEW YORK BOSTON

IT'S A PRISM!
IT BENDS LIGHT AND MAKES RAINBOWS!

LIGHT is made up of tiny little things called photons that are launched from the sun, light bulbs, screens, and anything else that produces light. Most light we see is called white light, but this "white light" is really a bunch of colors of light mixed together!

A glass prism bends light, but it bends some colors more than others. White light goes in one side of the prism and comes out the other side separated into a rainbow!

LIGHT

PRISM

RED
ORANGE
YELLOW

GREEN
BLUE
VIOLET

			VISIBLE LIGHT			
GAMMA RAYS	X-RAYS	ULTRAVIOLET LIGHT		INFRARED LIGHT	MICROWAVES	RADIO WAVES

The range of light our eyes can see is called visible light, but there are also colors of light that our eyes can't see!

Some birds and insects can see ultraviolet light, and some snakes and fish can sense infrared light. And radios "see" another kind of light called radio waves!

WHAT'S AT THE END OF A RAINBOW?

Sadly, nothing! Rainbows don't have an end—in fact, the ends would connect to make a circle if the ground wasn't in the way. A rainbow is just an illusion, caused by raindrops acting as tiny prisms bending and separating light toward your eyes. If you move toward a rainbow, it will appear to move, too. But if you're lucky enough to see a rainbow while high up in an airplane, you might be able to see a whole circle!

CAN PRISMS WORK BACKWARD?

In 1666, a scientist named Isaac Newton proved that white light is made of colored light. He used one prism to separate the light and then another to put it back together!

STRANGE-BOW! The sun's light contains all the colors of a rainbow, but most light bulbs don't. If you try shining different kinds of light through a prism, you'll see different rainbows on the other side!

IT'S A MAGNIFYING GLASS!

IT MAKES THINGS LOOK BIGGER!

The glass part of a magnifying glass is called a LENS. When light goes through clear things like glass, it bends toward the thickest part. In a magnifying glass, the thickest part is the center, so the light comes out aimed, or focused, toward a smaller area. When you look through it, it makes the stuff on the other side appear bigger!

LENSES CAN BE MANY SHAPES!

If the middle of a lens is thick, the light will bend a lot and come together close to the lens. The flatter the lens, the longer the distance before the light comes together. And if the middle of the lens is thinner than the edge, the light doesn't come together at all—it spreads out!

YOUR EYE HAS A LENS, TOO!

At the front of each eyeball, you have a natural lens. When light enters your eye, your lens bends it. The light comes together at the retina, a layer of cells inside your eyeball that responds to light. The retina sends your brain information about what it senses, and your brain organizes that into images.

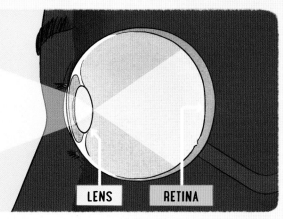

LENS   RETINA

50s CE

People have known that light bends in glass for at least 2000 years, but the first person to use a lens to see better may have been the Roman emperor Nero. It's believed he used a curved emerald to watch shows at the Colosseum.

1000s CE

Some people in medieval times used simple lenses called reading stones. They were half-spheres of glass and had to be placed right on top of the letters that needed to be magnified.

1200s CE

In Italy, people began attaching two lenses together, one for each eye—the first glasses! But even then, they were so rare and expensive that only the richest people could afford them.

1780s CE

Eventually people learned to attach lenses to other lenses, creating glasses that help you see close or far away, depending on which part you look through.

IN A FLASH! Light might seem instant to us, but it's not. It's just really, really fast—it can travel 186,000 miles every second! But even at that speed, it takes the sun's light eight minutes to reach us.

THEY'RE CRAYONS!

THEY'RE FOR DRAWING COLORS!

We don't actually see objects. We just see the light that bounces off them and into our eyes. But most things don't reflect ALL light—they only reflect SOME colors of light and absorb the rest.

If something reflects all colors, it looks white. If it absorbs all colors, it looks black. If it reflects only one color, it looks like that color. And if it reflects only a couple of colors, it looks like a mix of those colors. Each color of crayon absorbs and reflects different colors of light!

HOW DO WE MAKE COLORS?

A **PIGMENT** is what gives a crayon its color. A pigment is made of something that reflects a certain color of light, ground into a powder. Then it's mixed with other materials to make it useable for drawing or painting.

In a crayon, pigment is mixed with wax. In paint, it's mixed with a liquid, like oil, and in many markers, it's mixed with water.

People have been grinding new things into pigments for tens of thousands of years, including dirt, rocks, plants, bugs, gemstones, metals, and more recently, chemicals from laboratories.

40,000 BCE

Most of the earliest pigments were different colors of dirt and clay, along with white chalk, gray ash, and black charcoal from fires.

3,000 BCE

Some blues, yellows, greens, and reds in ancient Egyptian paintings were made from crushed rocks and minerals. Some, especially the reds and yellows, were poisonous!

100 BCE

Colors that are rare in nature, like blue and purple, were often the most expensive. One early chemical pigment, Han purple, was made by heating and mixing minerals and chemicals.

1750s CE

As distant countries traded more frequently, one paint palette might have included Indian yellow, Prussian blue, and even a brownish color made from real mummies.

1950s CE

Modern chemistry has led to a huge explosion of new colors in the past 200 years, giving artists all over the world access to bolder colors than ever before.

COLORFUL UNIVERSE! Different substances reflect different colors of light. One way astronomers guess what distant planets are made of is by studying how much of each color they reflect!

IT'S A CAMERA!

IT'S FOR TAKING PICTURES!

A modern camera has one or more lenses, a sensor, and a computer inside. The lens aims, or focuses, light toward the sensor, which can tell what colors of light are hitting it. When you take a picture, the computer records what the sensor is "seeing" right at that moment and saves it as an image!

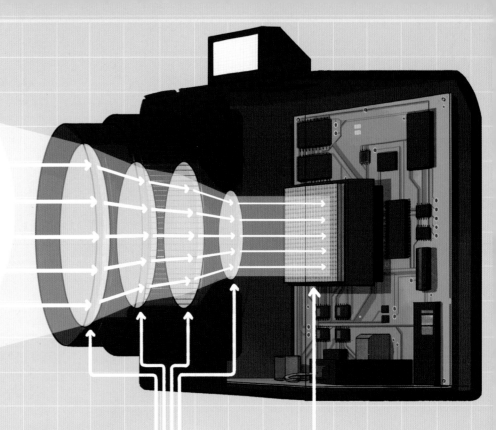

LENSES   SENSOR

1840s CE

Instead of sensors, the first cameras used metal plates that changed color where light hit them. You'd have to hold the camera still for several minutes to take a picture, and the images only came out in shades of black, white, and gray.

1890s CE

Later cameras used thin, flexible film instead of metal plates. Some types of film could react with light so fast that they could capture pictures of moving things. Then you'd send the film to a factory, where it would be used to put your pictures on paper.

1950s CE

By the 1950s, you could buy cameras and film that made pictures in full color, with lenses that could take photos of things far away or very, very close. And instead of sending your film away to be developed, you could just leave it at a local drugstore.

1980s CE

The first cameras to use sensors and computers instead of film let you see your pictures almost instantly—first on a computer, then in the 1990s, right on a camera screen. But the pictures on the screen were not sharp until later models.

2010s CE

Cameras used to be very expensive objects, but now you'll find one in every smartphone. Taking pictures, editing them, and sending them around the world can happen within seconds.

TIME TO SMILE! The metal plates in early cameras needed a lot of light to record an image, which meant it could take several minutes to make one picture. No wonder people in old pictures look so serious . . . . Try sitting perfectly still for *that* long!

IT'S A TV SCREEN!

IT SHOWS MOVING PICTURES!

A TV screen makes images out of thousands of red, green, and blue dots called PIXELS. The pixels are so tiny that your eye can't tell them apart—instead, it blurs them into an image!

But a screen doesn't just show one picture. It shows a bunch—60 or more every second—moving so fast that you can't tell them apart, and they blend together into what appears to be motion.

RED, GREEN, AND BLUE?

You can mix colors of light together into new colors just like with paint. But while the primary paint colors are red, yellow, and blue, the primary colors of light are red, green, and blue, and they don't all mix together in exactly the same way! For example, red and green light doesn't make brown—it makes yellow or orange, depending on how bright each light is.

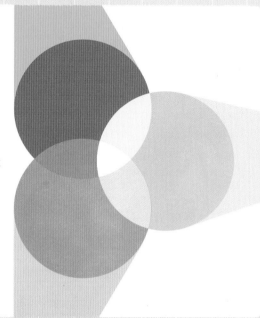

HOW CAN PICTURES MOVE?

Your eyes sense light, and your brain turns that light into images you can understand. But it's not perfect. Your brain can only make sense of around 10 images every second, and then fills in the gaps between them with what it *expects* to see. If your friend waves at you, your brain sees a hand in one position, and then sees it in another position, and assumes the hand moved. If you're looking at a flipbook or a TV screen, your brain does the same thing!

1930s CE   1950s CE   1980s CE   2010s CE

The first TV screens were big boxes with tiny, blurry screens. Instead of being made up of red, green, and blue dots, these screens could only show black-and-white pictures. Over the years, people found ways to make bigger and brighter screens, screens that could respond to touch, and screens small enough to fit in your pocket.

BIG LITTLE SCREEN! Some modern screens have more than 33 million pixels. If each pixel were just one inch across, that screen would be twice as long as a football field!

AUTHOR'S NOTE

This is a work of informational fiction. Anything that you learn from our child character is accurate. But beware the wacky Invention Hunters—almost nothing they say or do is wise, correct, or even possible!

Some concepts, dates, and diagrams have been generalized and simplified for ease of sharing and communicating to children. Where possible, illustrations are based on historical images, but in some cases where no visual record could be found, reasonable artistic license may have been used.

Special thanks to Elizabeth Segal for checking the facts.